Jane Hissey

Little Bear
and the
Silver Star

D0532784

04659453

IT was Christmas Eve and Old Bear and the other toys were busy decorating the Christmas tree.

'Little Bear,' said Rabbit, 'why are you dressed as a fairy?'

'I'm the Christmas tree fairy,' said Little Bear. 'We need something special for the top of the tree.'

'I'VE got a special bone,' said Ruff. 'You could use that?'
'I don't think a bone would look right,' grumbled Duck.
'Not on top of the tree.'
'You can use my special red scarf?' said Jolly Tall.
'Thank you, Jolly,' said Old Bear, 'but what we really
need is the silver star.'

'Oh, the star!' cried Little Bear. 'That's the special thing for
the top of the tree. Where is it?'

'In the attic, I think,' said Old Bear. 'But it's a bit late to
get it now. Perhaps another day.'

'BUT there *isn't* another day!' cried Little Bear. 'It's Christmas Day tomorrow!'

'Well,' said Old Bear kindly, 'maybe in the morning we'll find something else to put on the tree?'

'I won't be able to sleep,' said Little Bear sadly, as he got into his pyjamas. 'I don't feel ready for Christmas. We always have the star at the top of the tree.'

But he was very tired and soon he, and all the other toys, were fast asleep.

IT was quite dark when Little Bear woke up. The others were still sleeping. He looked across at the Christmas tree and suddenly remembered the star.

'If I climb up the tree now,' he said to himself, 'I could get to the attic and find it and everyone would be so happy in the morning!'

HE picked up a tiny lantern and began to climb the tree.
'I must be quick,' he said to himself, 'I have to be back in
bed before Father Christmas comes.'

It seemed a long way up, but at last he was at the very top
branch. He could just open the attic trapdoor and, with a big
heave, he pulled himself inside.

IT was very dark in the attic. Bravely, Little Bear held up his lantern and began to search for the star. He looked in things and under things and behind things.

'I don't know where it can be,' he sighed. Then he saw, in the light of his lantern, something sparkly on the floor.

'The star!' he cried, as he picked it up and hugged it.

'I knew I'd find it.'

JUST then he heard a muffled noise above his head.
It sounded like footsteps on the roof.

'Father Christmas!' he gasped.

He hurried to the little attic window and peered out.
But the window was all white; he couldn't see
anything at all.

'It's snowed,' he cried. 'Just in time for Christmas.'

H<small>E</small> pushed open the window for a better look and...
Whoosh!

A heap of snow rushed down the roof, picked him up and carried him all the way to the gutter.

Little Bear struggled to get out but he was stuck, right up to his middle, in the snow. And he couldn't see the star anywhere.

'Help!' he cried. 'Somebody help!'

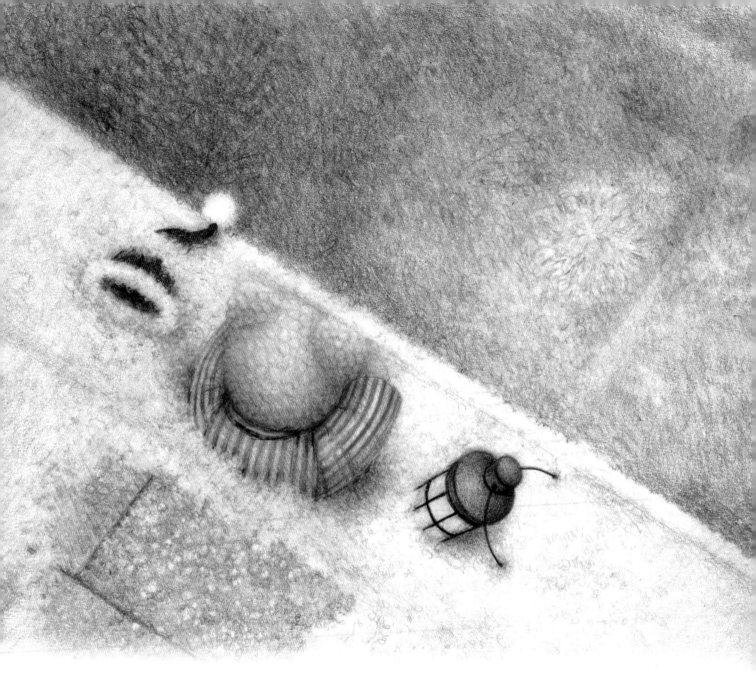

ALL was quiet. Little Bear felt very lonely. He wished he was still tucked up in bed, not sitting on the roof, in the snow, in his pyjamas, with no silver star.

Just then, something white flew out of the attic window
and landed beside him in the snow.

'An angel,' whispered Little Bear, peeping out from
behind his paws.

Then he saw that it wasn't an angel after all; it was
Hoot the owl.

'OH HOOT!' cried Little Bear. 'I'm so glad to see you.'

'Little Bear!' she said, as she pulled him out of the snow.
'I heard you calling. What are you doing out here?'

Little Bear told her about the footsteps, the snow and the
silver star. 'But now I've lost it again,' he sniffed, 'and if I
don't get back to bed soon I'll miss Father Christmas too.'

'Come on then,' said Hoot, 'I'll soon fly you back to bed.'

LITTLE BEAR scrambled onto Hoot's back and she flew up into the sky.

As they glided over the house, Little Bear looked down and gave a cry.

'Hoot, look, footprints on the roof; I *did* hear Father Christmas!'

He leaned over for a closer look.

'Hold on tight,' called Hoot, but it was too late; Little Bear toppled off and disappeared down the chimney.

B<small>ACK</small> in the playroom, all the toys had woken
up and were searching for Little Bear.
  'He must be around somewhere,' said Bramwell,
'his trousers are here.'

'No pyjamas though,' muttered Duck, 'and he hasn't opened any of his presents.'

AT that moment, they heard a funny noise coming from the fireplace. Jolly stuck his head up the chimney and who should he find, all covered in soot, but Little Bear.

'Little Bear,' cried the other toys. 'What were you doing in there?'

Little Bear told them about his adventure and how he'd found the missing star.

'I wanted to surprise everyone,' he sniffed, 'but now I've lost it again.'

'IT was a very brave and kind thing to do,' said Old Bear, giving Little Bear a hug.

Then Bramwell noticed something lying in the fireplace: a funny-shaped parcel tied up with ribbon. It said 'For Little Bear' on the label.

'This must be for you,' he said, handing it to Little Bear.

LITTLE BEAR tore open the paper and there, inside, was the silver star; all shiny and ready for Christmas.

'The star,' gasped Little Bear. 'But I lost it in the snow?'

'Well, I wonder who found it?' laughed Hoot as she swooped down to join them.

'Come on, Little Bear, let's put it on top of the tree where it belongs.'

Little Bear climbed onto Hoot's back and they flew up in the air.

'Happy Christmas everyone!' he called.

'Happy, *sparkly* Christmas!'

For Laurie

SALARIYA
SCRIBO BOOK HOUSE SCRIBBLERS

This edition published in Great Britain in MMXXI by Scribblers,
an imprint of The Salariya Book Company Ltd
25 Marlborough Place,
Brighton BN1 1UB

www.salariya.com
www.janehissey.co.uk

© The Salariya Book Company Ltd MMXXI
Text and illustrations © Jane Hissey MMXXI

All rights reserved. No part of this publication may be reproduced, stored in or introduced into a retrieval system or
transmitted in any form, or by any means (electronic, mechanical, photocopying, recording or otherwise) without the
written permission of the publisher. Any person who does any unauthorised act in relation to this publication may be
liable to criminal prosecution and civil claims for damages.

PB ISBN-13: 978-1-913337-44-5

1 3 5 7 9 8 6 4 2

A CIP catalogue record for this book is available from the British Library.

Printed and bound in China.
Printed on paper from sustainable sources.

This book is sold subject to the conditions that it shall not, by way of trade or otherwise, be lent, resold, hired out, or
otherwise circulated without the publisher's prior consent in any form or binding or cover other than that in which it
is published and without similar condition being imposed on the subsequent purchaser.